MOON SLAYER

THE RETURN OF THE LIONS OF DURGA

THE SECOND BOOK OF KOKORO

AN ILLUSTRATED STORY BY

NEIL HAGUE

Quester

First published in 2015 by
Quester Publications
www.neilhague.com

Cover Design: Neil Hague

British Library Cataloguing-in Publication Data
A catalogue record for this book is
available from the British Library

ISBN 0-9541904-7-7

Printed by Lightning Source

"Love is a river of life in the world"
Henry Ward Beecher

A big thank you to Ellis for his unwavering support for my work over the years and for having an acute eye for detail when it comes to the subjects contained within this book.

Thank you to 'all of you' that have blessed me with your friendship, inspiration and wisdom over the past 20 years. The book your about to read wouldn't be here if it wasn't for friends such as Mel, David and the many 'Facebook friends' that connect with me through this type of material.
Thank you also to Patrick for hours of 'esoteric' conversations in the National Portrait Gallery Cafe over the years.

Peace be with you all.

I dedicate this book to the 'human imagination'.
It lives forever...

"I rest not from my great task!
To open the Eternal Worlds, to open the Immortal Eyes
Of Man inwards into the Worlds of Thought, into Eternity
Ever expanding in the Bosom of God, the Human Imagination."
William Blake, *Jerusalem*

"For once you have tasted flight you will walk the earth with your eyes
turned skywards, for there you have been
and there you will long to return."
Leonardo da Vinci

"Everything you can imagine is real."
Pablo Picasso

"Imagination is the beginning of creation. You imagine what you desire,
you will what you imagine and at last you create what you will."
George Bernard Shaw

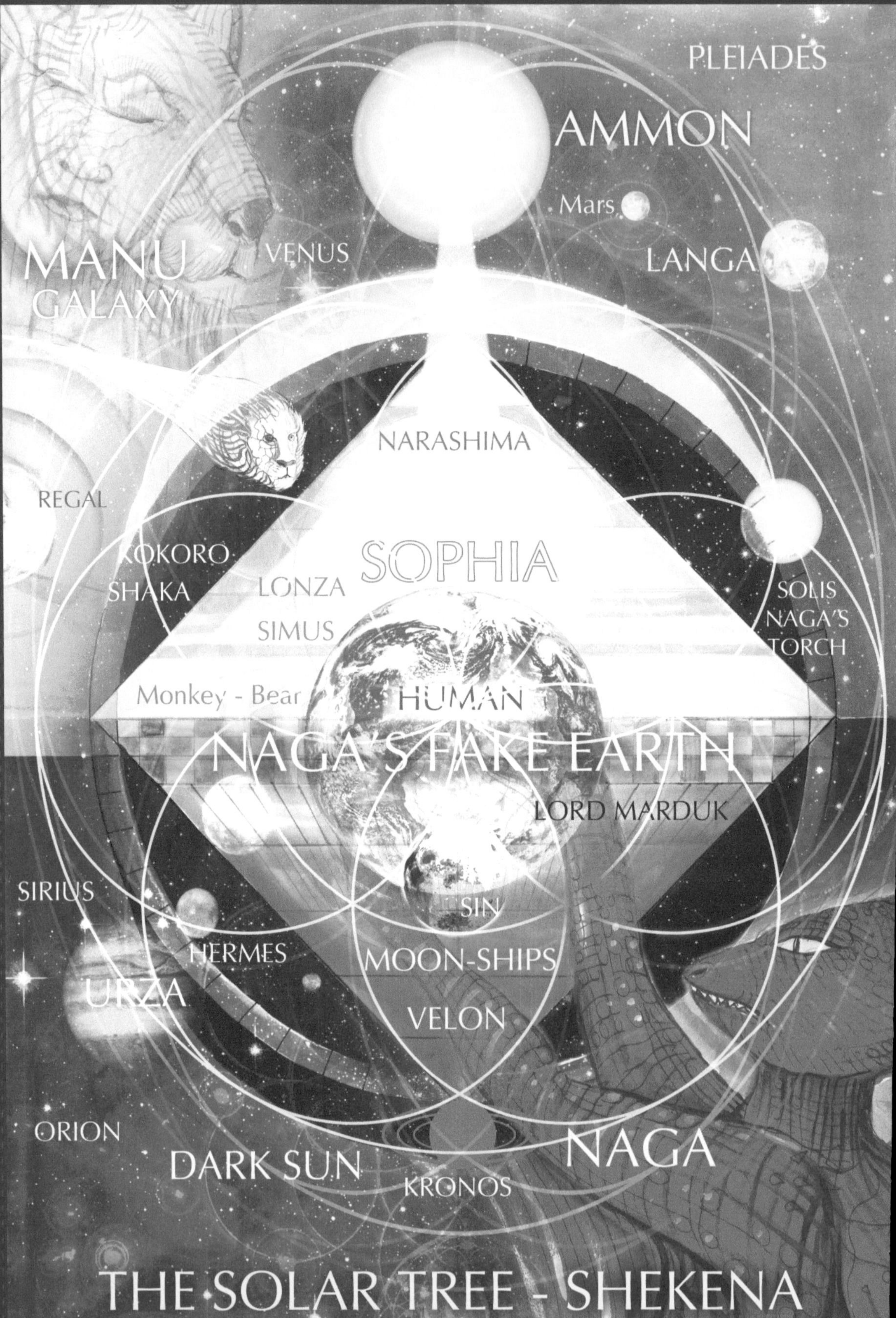

THE SOLAR TREE - SHEKENA

Introduction: THE LOGOS OF DURGA

"Mother of Gods, Father of Gods, the Old God,
distend in the navel of the earth,
engaged in the enclosure of turquoise,
he who dwells in the waters the colour of the bluebird"

Nahuatl Hym - God Ometeoll

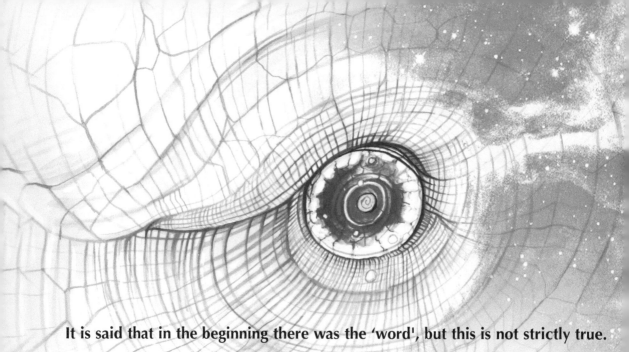

It is said that in the beginning there was the 'word', but this is not strictly true.

nstead, there was a 'deep longing' an 'immense thought' that became the *'word'*. The longing was called the *'logos'* and it was more than just a thought, it was an incredible 'act of creation', a desire to manifest life through the infinite imagination - *infinite Oneness*. The logos was an act of *Oneness* made visible through a 'divine form' called Durga. Moved with compassion for those that could not see what she saw, the goddess Durga gave life to thousands of galaxies and stars. She 'imagined' them into existence.

She was a faceless celestial goddess and the creator of our Galaxy. When seen in our world she took the form of a lion's eye, not an ordinary eye, but one that churned like an endless blue sea of fire, crystal-like, yellow and turquoise in colour. Inside her eye was a sea of 'fire stones' that were the most precious stones in the Universe. An immense love and power came from Durga and the divine forms that took shape through the thoughts and dreams of the one they called the Queen of the Lions. Durga's eye was a mass of crystal plasma a place where black holes, like small pebbles, became encircled by a raging celestial fire that dazzled in the darkness of space. There was 'no time' in this place, just the endless Universe. The eye of Durga shone, as a beacon for all that was true, just, righteous and *infinite*.

Each star system that came out of this eye was a living 'being of light' and each point of light got its source of power from a celestial river that revolved around the Eye of Durga. Our Galaxy came out of Durga and its name was Manu, part-lion, part human, he was the *first* 'divine human form'.

Like all galaxies created by Durga, Manu radiated the original fire source and the 'stones' that give life to all stars and suns. Manu was a creator in his own right and from him would come the many stars and suns that 'spiralled' out of his heart and mind. As Manu grew, he

Manu is born of Durga.

Naga is born of Manu.

shifted form and birthed ideas that became star systems. He also doubted his own creative power. Manu's doubt one day gave form to something that would challenge the worlds that Manu had created.

It was in the 'time of creation', or the time of the 'first world', when a great serpent called Naga emerged from the mind and the body of Manu. The emergence was called the 'splitting of the divine being' an event that many ancients would record in art and stories across the millenniums that would pass. Naga was born of the original source that gave life to Manu and as a creator god he too would shape worlds in *his* own image. This great red dragon wanted more than anything to create a world that was for himself - his own creation. Like particles of dust in sunlight, worlds were formed through thought as Naga used his mind to shape 'worlds of light' that we now call planets. Naga, being part of Durga and Manu, could cast spells and make magic, and doing so, crafted worlds called timeships. But having been born of doubt he

9

had a darker side, a side that would create havoc eventually.

As Naga beat his wings moving energy 'matter', he shaped a ball of light creating a perfect time-ship that he looked upon with delight. Naga called his creation Sophia, a place where human beings would emerge and come to live, a place that would be also called Earth. Naga moved Sophia across the heavens to a place called Shekena - the great Solar Tree, or what we today call the Solar System. Created by Manu, these Solar Trees were born just as babies are born in our world, and they would grow to take the form of Solar beings, giving life themselves to other planets and satellites. When Sophia arrived in Shekena, it was a very different place to what it is today. Many 'creators' came and took the form of planets that moved across the vastness of Shekena's body. They were called the 'wanderers of old' and some even challenged each other for a central

position within the Solar Tree. The Age of the Planets had begun.

Naga's Earth became a place of intrigue by the wanderers that came to visit Shekena in this region of the Galaxy. Creators from constellations such as the Pleiades, Orion and

The Eye of Manu giving life to Shekena and other Solar Systems.

Sirius were attracted to Sophia. Some also left their 'seed' on Earth and not before long the Earth was like a 'star garden' that grew to become known as the 'Garden of Earthly Delights'. As the garden grew it became the attraction to other 'beings' from neighbouring planets, others came from further away across the great body of Manu. But Naga watched them all closely monitoring his time-ship Earth. So it was, from the 'mind and hands' of Naga and the 'body of Manu' came to grow a beautiful creation - a goddess in her own right. Sophia and her 'Garden of Earthly Delights' became the star attraction everyone looked towards.

Sophia admired by the gods' and star tribes

Sophia and her 'Garden of Earthly Delights'

Humanity at this time were not as we 'see ourselves' today. They were more 'non physical', luminous and could travel great distances without moving their bodies. Amazing people lived in the 'Garden of Earthly Delights'. Star people, Bear people (called Simus), monkey people and also the 'giant offspring' of Naga, (the dinosaurs), all lived in the garden. All of these creatures, animals and humans lived in the garden at the same time, which had the same warm climate all over the Earth. Sophia had not wandered across the Solar Tree of Shekena, she shone from a location between the Pleiades and a Sun called Langa a beautiful maiden whose name meant to 'long for'. Langa, the daughter of Manu, was a 'distant sun' but she was a dear friend (a distant cousin) to Sophia. Both Sophia and Langa were truly beautiful goddesses.

In the garden on Sophia there were also 'creatures' that walked amongst the 'first people' as 'gods', and it was these 'non-physical beings' that taught humans about the *Dreamtime* and their connection to

The Simus tribes protect the Earth.

Manu and Durga. Others that came were 'beings of light' (angels), and just as bees and butterflies visit the most beautiful of gardens, they came so to spread their knowledge and wisdom too. The garden

The 'First People' of Sophia.

The Garden of Sophia.

was nurtured and loved by the first people of Earth and harmony, peace and creativity abounded at this time. Sophia loved her people and in return, they too gave love to their goddess. As Sophia evolved and shone, the offspring of Naga decreased in number, until over time they had almost totally disappeared. Naga's time-ship became a golden colour 'shining' like the brightest star across the heavens. However, what seemed to be the most beautiful creation was soon looked upon with envious eyes that lurked in the darkest regions of our Galaxy. Naga had not forgotten his part in the original creation of Sophia and wanted what he perceived to be his daughter. His desire grew and his eyes were fixed on her more vehemently as time passed by. Like an alpha predator fixes on its prey he coveted her magnetism and beauty to attract other beings. He began to hate her and with *his* eye on the many planets in the Solar Tree, he decided the time had come to claim his rightful position and take back his Earth.

The Simus held the
light of Langa on their
staffs and watched
over Sophia.

AMMON

Part One: THE FALL
200,000 to 35,001 BC

"Placed in the order of the stars, when the five senses whelmed
In deluge o'er the earth-born man: then bound the flexile eyes
Into two stationary orbs concentrating all things:
The ever-varying spiral ascents to the heaven of heavens
Were bended downward, and the nostril's golden gates shut,
Turned outward, barred and petrified against the infinite.
Thought changed the infinite to a serpent; that which pitieth
To a devouring flame; and man fled from its face and hid
In forests of night; then all the eternal forests were divided
Into earths rolling in circles of space, that like an ocean rushed
And overwhelmed all except this finite wall of flesh.
Then was the serpent temple formed, image of (the) infinite
Shut up in finite revolutions, and man became an Angel;
Heaven a mighty circle turning; God a tyrant crowned."

William Blake

As Naga's desire for Sophia grew, a bright young star had also moved into the Solar Tree of Shekena. The ancients knew its name as Ammon the Hero. In time it became a great 'father figure' to the planet we call Earth. Naga had also watched this star with interest and envied Ammon's glow and love for him by other wanderers that crossed the sphere of the Solar System. Ammon was huge compared to Langa and he formed a great 'pillar of light' that led, like a stairway, to the centre of a bright orb. He was known as the 'Pole God' and became a 'second', but much bigger sun for Sophia. As Langa moved back towards her original Solar Tree, (the Pleiades), Ammon became the focus for Sophia. From Ammon's centre flowed a celestial river in 'four directions' ablaze with the light of Manu. The four directions became symbolized as the four races of Earth, Red and Yellow, Black and White as they migrated across Sophia's body following the light of Ammon. The people of Sophia Earth grew to love this young male Sun and many a home and city was dedicated to the one they called Father. All Earth circles, communities, mounds and settlements come from the memory of Ammon's reign over a very different Earth to the one we know today.

At this time, freewill prevented other gods from enthroning another creator or destroying what other creators had created. The truth of the Eye of Durga watched over all that lived in the light of the Galaxy. But, just as Naga envied Sophia, he also grew tired of this 'young sun god', becoming ever more irritated by Ammon's people of the now golden Earth, he decided it was time to reclaim his creation.

Ammon Arrives.

Naga decided to return to the source of all stars himself and steal fire from the eye of the mighty Goddess Durga. Only with her fire could he reclaim his Earth and banish Ammon from his place in the Solar Tree. Naga travelled great distances beyond the speed of light moving through time and space until he had reached the central fire of Durga. Using his magic to deceive the goddess by becoming invisible to her sight, he turned 'one eye' into a 'terrible stone'

Naga steals the 'fire stone'.

Naga creates the Demiurge out of the face of Durga.

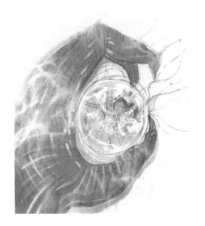

that would become the focus of his distorted desires. Naga had created a 'key' into another world. From this world a terrible god appeared, a combination of Naga and Durga, part-lion, part-serpent, peering through the key. Naga's act of 'deception' created a schism called the Demiurge, a 'self-aware distortion' of the true light of Durga.

As the face of the Demiurge formed, Naga then reached into the fire and took a stone from the Eye of Durga, one of the many stones that were used to create planets and suns. And so it was, Naga now held a 'fire stone' in his hand while he made haste back to Shekena and the Earth he had created. Naga would become the 'light bearer' mentioned by those that would later survive what he set in motion and as he entered the realm of Ammon he cast a shadow of darkness over the Golden Earth. Using the fire that he now held like a torch, Naga's flame appeared as a new Sun in the sky moving nearer to Sophia. And so began the time of the 'Fallen Sun' and the 'Sun that moves'. For the first people of Earth it was the 'first time' they had 'felt fear' and felt 'threatened' by those that moved in the 'shadows'. Naga's torch was a new light; a beacon of false hope and with these two Suns seen in the sky (Ammon and

Naga brings *his* Sun to Shekena.

the Torch of Naga) the people of Earth became confused and no longer looked at Ammon in the same way…and neither were they prepared for what happened next!

Empowered by the distortion that had occurred in the face of Durga, the 'great red serpent' grew in size. Expanding his body, he rose to place *his* fire stone in front of Ammon. With this fire he transformed the light of Ammon into a lesser light. Ammon was now possessed by the envy and rage of Naga and Sophia's people looked on in horror as Ammon's brilliance

The rotating crescent of Ammon
seen from Sophia

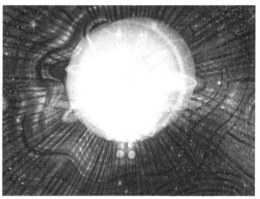

Ammon is Possessed by Naga, who also births moons.

was overshadowed. Days turned to nights, and weeks turned into months, as Naga 'emerged' from the body of Ammon to create a 'false light', a 'lesser Sun', who's light became a 'cold light' of a world now descending into chaos.

The alien sun cast its pall over the light of Ammon while a matrix spun from threads that emerged from the back of Naga imprisoned the beautiful Sophia. Naga banished Ammon leaving his light to fade and his body to drift into darkness. The convergence of these two celestial bodies became known as the 'Fallen Sun' or the 'Dark Sun', whose disc became encircled by a rotating crescent of light. This new Sun could be seen at night, as well as in

the day by the people of Sophia. As Naga become more rampant in his desire to drive out Ammon's light, he entered the heart of Ammon and possessed what was left of this Sun for himself. Naga's body became enraged and as he emerged he sent out waves from his body like ripples around a stone thrown into a celestial lake. Naga had brought chaos to the Solar System; and while *his* torch light stolen from Durga shone above the Earth as a new Sun distracting those that dwelt in its light by day, by night, this great serpent forged bands or revolving islands congealed around *his* 'new sun'. Naga had found a new abode, a perfect place to breed new forms that would follow his command. The bands around Naga appeared as well-formed geometrically unified 'rings', a new celestial mass, and the world slowly

The Velon and Kilipoth
are sent out to take Sophia.

21

became darker. Naga had birthed a 'new era', and created another Sun. He called his sun Kronos and from it came a new 'life form', one that lived 'artificially' and had no energy of its own.

The All-Seeing Eye of Kronos.

'Let There Be Light' – Naga's False Light

From the centre of the newly constructed Kronos a great cry went out, 'silent' but felt by all those in its vicinity. Naga had become a terrible eye, a combination of Ammon, Durga and himself. With his eye ablaze he gave birth to a race of machines half-serpent half-cyborg, all replicas of the pain caused by the merging of the two suns. The minions of Naga were known as the Kilipoth, the Velon, or the Archon (collectively as the Elohim). These entities had no consciousness (life source) of their own. They were 'living machines', the first vampires, whose life force was forged through the theft of the fire of Durga causing the Demiurge to appear. By nature the life

forms that spewed out from Naga's new Sun' Kronos were parasites and they were the children of the coupling of Ammon's shrinking light and the invisible light of the new 'Dark Sun'.

The Elohim breathed out artificial consciousness, in the form of 'boxes of restriction'. These 'cubes of confinement' travelled across 'space and time' and acted as the 'force field' for Naga to craft his next creation, the matrix – the *new* False Earth. Naga's matrix of light was so powerful that it would eventually threaten the freedom of

Naga's Demiurge.

every life form within the original 'Garden of Earth'. Sophia was doomed!

The Velon were huge serpent deities that became known as the 'five gods' or the five pillars, their purpose was to *restrict* the 'senses' of humanity. Part-Naga, part-cyborg, the Velon breathed out 'boxes of control', green invisible cubes and at the same time they 'sucked in energy', or life force, from the surrounding planets and stars that they fell upon. Like parasitical machines 'devouring' and 'spinning' a vast 'web of light', their other purpose was to wipe out the memory of the Golden Age of Sophia. As the Velon flew out across the Solar Tree, Naga bellowed from his Dark Sun, *"Let there be Light* [his light] *and there was light"*. And so it was, Naga's 'new world' came into existence.

Ammon was no more; instead Naga's Dark Sun Kronos corrupted and preyed upon the surrounding planets. A new 'Earth Matrix' was given life by Naga's light and this took the form of a 'fake Earth' a bad copy of Sophia. The arrival of his fake *new* Earth heralded the time of the 'all-seeing eye', 'Naga's eye', a 'mainframe' that would 'keep time', and watch over *all* that dwelled in the Solar Tree.

Nagas's theft of the fire stone of Durga and possession of Ammon had caused a terrible schism in the very fabric of our Galaxy, and from it came much pain, suffering and division, not least felt by the beings that we call planets.

But all was not what it seemed. Even though a Demiurge had been created by Naga's 'treason', the fire of Durga was stir-

ring due to this theft. The *infinite* had felt a disturbance at the centre of its own body. The balance now unsettled, other forces were 'mobilizing' in response to Naga's theft and possession. Durga was awakening and so would the lions of Regal.

The Schism on Sophia (Earth).

23

Part Two: WHEN THE MOON CAME

35,001 to 9,000 BC

"Then rose the seed of Chaos and of Night
To Blot out order and extinguish light.
Of dull and venal a new world to mould,
And bring Saturnian days of lead and gold"
POPE: Dunicad, IV, 13

"In one night the Atlantic Continent was caught up with the Moon,
And became an opaque Globe far distant clad with moony beams.
The visions of Eternity, by reason of narrowed perceptions,
are become weak visions of time and space, fixed into furrows of death:
Til deep dissimulation is the only defence an honest man has left..."
William Blake - *Jerusalem*. plate 49

A s Ammon was transformed into Kronos, many satellites known as Moons were sucked in and spewed out by the vast magnetic force of the Naga's newly generated Dark Sun. Some moons were once planets in their own right, with their people banished from the surface, the remnants of 'galactic' battles between different stellar intelligences. One star system called Draco, another creation of Naga, waged war across several planets and Moons against a part-human, part-bird species from the Pleiades. Helped by Naga himself the Dragons of Draco took many Moons. Some Moons were hollowed out 'space stations' that became 'ghost ships' wandering across the 'sea of space', used by star people such as Naga's Draco to change and monitor other worlds. Arriving from Kronos and other spheres and driven by the Elohim, (Archon and Velon), some of these moons would cause mayhem to worlds that would otherwise live in balance and harmony.

Moons born of Kronos.

The Velon and Archons were 'creators in their own way, not by imagination, but by 'mimicking' other's creations. They were called the 'Children of the Schism', and with their own minds they fashioned a God in the 'image' of their creator, but gave him the appearance of the human race that they now pursued. Their creation was called Lord Marduk - the God-King, a deity that would forever punish the 'people of Earth'.

The Battle for Moon-ship Sin.

Marduk Rises.

As Moons were being sent out and planets fought over, Marduk had risen out of the vibration and dark matter of the newly forming rings of Kronos.

As battles took place in the Solar System, Naga's avaricious ambition reached out to take possession of ships, satellites and other planets. As he caused planets to clash and others to be destroyed his spirit possessed one particular moon which had caught the attention of his baleful eye. This bright satellite that came to haunt our night became a vessel for the Naga-Velon-Marduk alliance as it anchored near to the new Earth. This Moon was called 'Sin' and its name became known for humanity's pain and suffering at the time of the 'fall of Ammon'. When the Moon Sin arrived *everything* changed.

Some moons and planets are living beings in their own right, others are the creation of Naga. Naga's moons' were birthed from the rings of 'fire and ice' created by an artificial consciousness that also held the great red serpent's new Earth Matrix in place. Naga's moons were space ships, or Arks, sent out from the rings of Kronos. 'Sin' was one of them. Moons like 'Sin' were designed to travel great distances across the Galaxy, but once taken by Naga and his Velon these vehicles became 'ghost ships'. Like pirate ships in our world, they would be used to 'hijack' and take over other planets desired by those that wanted the planet's resources.

Just as reptiles lay their eggs, these 'moon-ship-eggs' were birthed and rolled into place under the 'new celestial order' of Naga. Like a parasite leaving its eggs, these moons were strategically moved into place across the 'web of space'. Sin, Earth's new

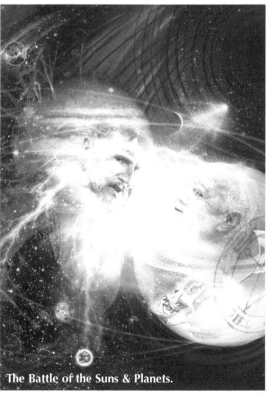
The Battle of the Suns & Planets.

Moon-ship Sin.

Ninurtra.

moon, was moved into its precise orbit by Naga's minions instructed according to the calculations of the Great Serpent; and calibrated to suck into its shadows and hollows the life force of everything that existed within its reach.

Inside Moon-ship Sin was a reptilian queen called Ninurtra. She was the daughter of Naga and one of three reptilian deities that came from the Draco constellation. A giant beyond comprehension in our world, Ninurtra was known by many names to the priesthoods that eventually would worship both her and Naga on Earth. To the ancients' priests of Naga's new Earth she became Istar, Ostara (Easter), Semiramis or the Goddess inside the Moon Egg.

Within the Moon were vast buildings, multi-levelled constructions and advanced technology that was as 'old as the stars' and built by 'ancient star tribes' – the descen-

dants of Manu. In the centre of Moon-ship Sin was Ninurtra, along with her children, the Nagas, whose name would eventually become the inspiration for *all* religious hierarchy on Naga's *new* Earth. It was said Ninurtra fed off gold and hoarded crystals taken from planets that were plundered by the Nagas.

With Ninurtra at the helm, and the Velon possessing the vehicle, just as planned Moon-ship Sin appeared out of nowhere. Nothing was the same on Earth again.

With the arrival of the Moon Sin, the Earth's magnetic field 'trembled' and her oceans emptied onto the land, like endless tears flowing from the face of one that loses something special, someone dear. Another 'schism' occurred in the newly arranged Solar System and the way had been prepared for a 'new world', one that would 'look and feel' very different to the original

Inside Moon-ship Sin.

garden of Sophia. The effect of the Moon's arrival caused a 'great flood', one that was eventually recorded in texts and told in stories by the civilizations that followed. The Earth 'turned over' and her energy fields were traumatized. Sophia's Earth 'matrix' was shaken creating canyons and ravines devastating the surface world and all that lived on it. When the seas eventually settled few original humans remained. The surface of the Earth was changed so much that no one alive would recognise Sophia. 'Paradise was lost' and with it the innocence of the original Earth too.

Marduk's Harvest

Led by Marduk, the Kilipoth and the Velon, the 'children of the serpent' arrived on the surface of a now traumatised Earth. Out of the darkness and chaos that ensued Marduk commanded his Velon armies to make slaves of Earth's people. While Ninurta prepared a 'new human seed' *inside* the laboratories on the Moon to be planted on the Earth, Marduk was given the task of removing what was left of the original population. From this 'seed', called Eve, would eventually come all kinds of 'kingships', 'Moon Archons' (Monarchs) and 'rulers' on the *new* Earth.

Like locusts the alliance of Marduk and Velon reptilian armies swarmed across the Earth. They caught many in their nets and those that escaped became outcasts and went underground into the caves of what

was left of Sophia. In the early days of the invasion a half-monkey, half-lion chief called Lonza, led an army of bears against the might of Marduk. They fought valiantly

30

The Velon-reptilian hunters arrive on Earth.

and used ancient magic in memory of their original Earth, but the powers of Marduk were too dark and too strong for them. Many survivors from the Lonza and Simus bear tribes were rounded up and made into slaves, others were taken away never to be seen again.

Lonza and the Simus fight Marduk for Earth.

Lonza fights the Demons of Naga.

Green Lion priest controls the Jeal through magic.

When Lonza saw the devastation caused at the hand of Marduk he retreated to his ancestral home in the stars. Once the armies of Marduk had taken the surface and the entire planet was ready, it was time to re-populate the Earth.

From the caves of the Earth came the first prototypes controlled by Marduk and Ninurtra from her strategically placed command base on the Moon. Out of places like the Blombos Cave and the 'Cradle of Life' in what we call Africa a new human form with a 'Naga brain', attuned to the 'memory of the Schism', was born out of the darkness of Naga's *new* Earth. Ninurta's *new* human being was genetically 'prepared' (ready-made) to accept the 'new Matrix of light' emitting from Naga's Dark Sun. Moon-ship Sin would be its anchor in the sky, like a gigantic computer (a super server) that administered the control of life on the *new* Earth. The world was taken! The old Earth (Sophia) was gone.

After thousands of years had passed, 'Original Sin' was 'conceived' and imposed on the people of the new Earth by the priests of Naga. These priests were called Jeal, half-wolf half-lion, and they served both Marduk and Naga. Like thieves that enter a house, the Jeal and Red Lions came to Earth through doorways (portals) in the 'fabric of time' created by Naga, so to administer his false 'matrix of light'. As the water receded after the flood, a vast army was also sent out across the Earth to 'police' Naga's *new* World Order. With armor like that of a beetle, all black and shiny, and led by the Bone Men, the Black Army of Kronos moved across the Earth removing what was left of the original light of Sophia. Genetically engineered humans became

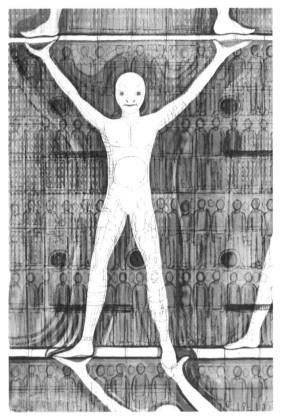

The Bone Men holding up Marduk's structure.

The Jeal watched by the Red Lions of Naga

'sheep' to the Jeal, who administrated humanity's newfound fears. Darkness was everywhere and with Naga's *new* hierarchy on Earth, from Red and Green Lions that watched over the Jeal, to the Bone Men, (who would hold in place the *'invisible'* hierarchical structure); the 'false' Earth was now complete. It was the beginning of the 'Empire of the Dark

Black Army of Kronos.

The Naga brain is perfected by Marduk.

Adam and Eve were created on Moon-ship Sin and their 'genetics' brought to the *new* Earth.

Sun', when *all* calendars were invented and implemented. When *all* temples were designed and the 'blueprint' for the 'new fake' Earth was laid out across the land like a vast web of illusion; It's patterns, shapes, symbols and 'beliefs' all 'pre-designed' and big enough to cover the *whole* Earth. From this blueprint *all* religion was born.

Part Three: THE TIME OF SHADOWS
9,000 BC - *to now*

*"Wantonly the old ones trod the ways of darkness and
their blasphemy was great upon the Earth"*
The Book of Dead Names – George Hay

O ver several more thousands years the great Pyramid temple cities were constructed by those that worshiped their new Sun Father God - Marduk. Ammon, and the Golden Age they once enjoyed, had faded into distant memory. Instead, strict laws and harsh commandments written in stone were imposed upon this 'new slave race' of Earth. With these laws and rules came 'human hybrid' rulers, leaders and the bloodlines of the Naga. Royal families were created out of the human hybrid population; and world leaders appointed in different locations called continents and countries so to ensure Marduk's control was fully operational *all over the Earth*. Even when leaders changed over the centuries, Marduk was always the real power behind each new leader.

And so it came to pass that inexorably the priesthoods of Naga and Ninurtra compelled the people to worship Marduk as their one and only true God. Their vicious missionary work knew no bounds; dire threats, terror, and murderous punishments and campaigns wore down and crippled the loving human spirit. For those that succumbed enough, to the priests' satisfaction, riches and status were awarded. To those who didn't came poverty, ceaseless slavery, and for those ordained suitable, a victimisation so terrible, so vile, so monstrous… so Marduk: 'human sacrifice'. What did the priests of the Great Serpents care; they'd always done it, and been at it since they first erupted, like boils, on Earth. Their crawling had served them well. They also knew well the subliminal power of symbols and frequencies in the 'art of control', and disseminated them in surreptitious and counterfeit vehicles everywhere that eyes

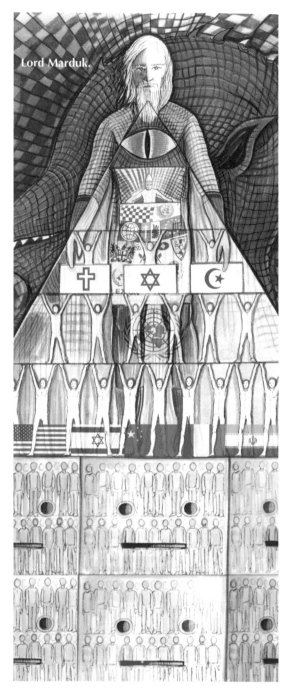

Lord Marduk.

and ears would fall upon them.

The priests of Marduk initiated a new hierarchy on Earth from Naga down to themselves, and through this, they would grow in strength, in secret, hidden from all those that gave their power to the 'artificial' 'blue print' of Marduk's World. A 'veil' came

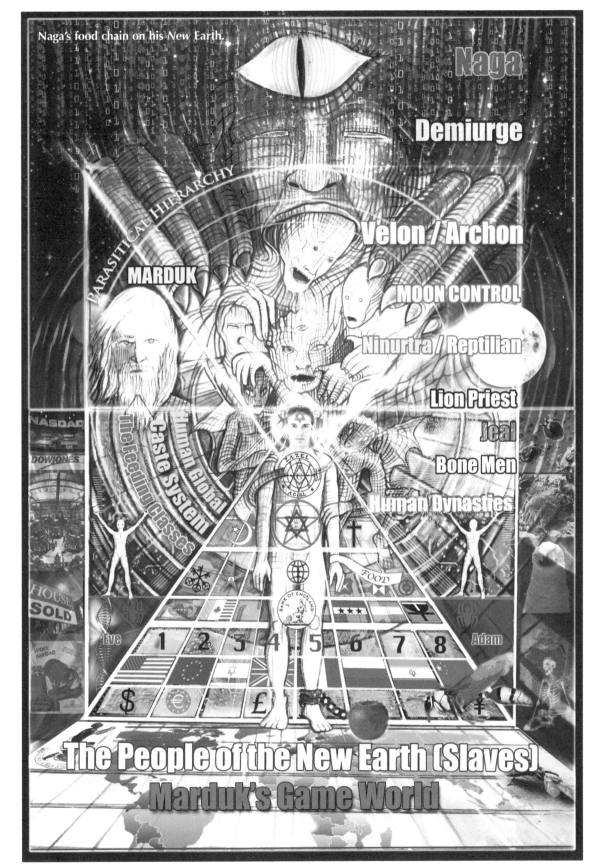

Naga's food chain on his New Earth.

Naga

Demiurge

PARASITICAL HIERARCHY

Velon / Archon

MARDUK

MOON CONTROL

Ninurtra / Reptilian

Lion Priest

Jeal

Bone Men

Human Dynasties

Human Global Caste System
The Feeding Classes

NASDAQ

DOW JONES

HOUSE SOLD

WORK ABROAD

Eve

1 2 3 4 5 6 7 8

Adam

$ € £ ¥

The People of the New Earth (Slaves)
Marduk's Game World

37

down over human sight and this hierarchy has not changed since the time of the 'fall', it just became more sophisticated as the millenniums passed. Now that the sublime human spirit of the original Earth had been subjugated they were blind to the presence of the Velon (Archon), Marduk, and the Bone Men; and they could not read the signs and symbols cast to control their impressions. All were 'invisible' to those that no longer saw in the ancient way. Locked in boxes of the mind, like bees in a hive, they were limited in their perception of all that there was to *see* and *know* beyond Naga's *new* Earth and Marduk's imposition. The time of the 'perception deception' was now here.

Artificial Reality forged by Kronos and the Moon.

REVOLUTION ON EARTH

Humanity in 'prisons' of the 'hive mind' of Naga

Naga's 'false light' is broadcast from Kronos - Saturn. It 'creates' the fake Earth.

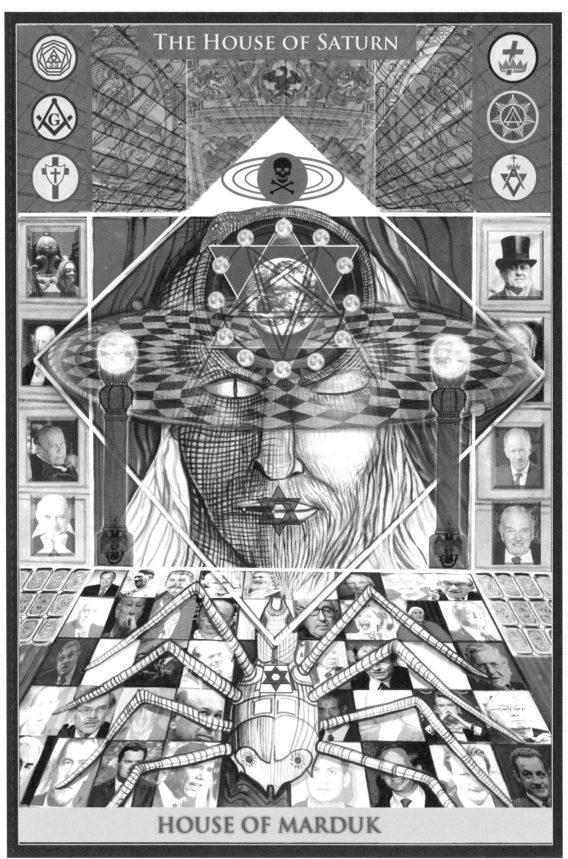

THE HOUSE OF SATURN

HOUSE OF MARDUK

The House of Marduk

After thousands of years, since Marduk had come to the new Earth, the priests of Naga and their unseen masters had ravished the surface world. They consumed the energy of all that was left of the true life force of those that remembered Sophia. Naga had created a 'Saturn world' in the image of the 'original schism', the original *separation*. Life under Naga's 'Dark Sun' and Marduk's imposition was reduced to a 'mechanical consciousness' feeding on an 'artificial' reality. All around, people had become 'star struck', while starving for inner peace and happiness in their hearts. Machines had become Earth's 'ancestors' and all unborn generations would be fed to the 'control machine-world'. The 'elite order' of Marduk, the 'House of Marduk', ruled the Earth, serving its master - Naga, the Demiurge and the Schism that created them *all*. Humans, once great and aware of who they were, had become a sleep walking race that even encouraged (and drove) their own children to be claimed and fashioned into food for this 'ever hungry' 'mechanical system'.

Inside the House of Marduk was a 'spider-like beast' that thrived by 'taking the energy' of 'the stock', the innocent and the vulnerable. All energy was first collected in temples but over time, with the increased exploitation of the Earth's body and life systems and life forms, the areas of specific responsibilities have diversified. Temples do what they have always done but other transmitters and receivers of Earth's energy are in operation too. On a par, and overtaking, are what have become known as 'stock exchanges'. The address of the London Stock exchange (for example), since 1801, is a tribute to Saturn, Paternoster Square - Paternoster being 'Our Father', a magical incantation, and also a fishing set-up incorporating lead - Saturn's metal. A square is another symbol for Saturn. The L.S.E is in the City of London, along with other formidable edifices of human subjugation; where it is attended by winged dragons (Draco) bearing Saturn's red cross. Their plinths are said to be made of Portland Stone. The City of London is a port indeed, but her ships sail to and from a harbour 'not of this world'. The epithet of the Bank of England (also in the City), the 'Old Lady of Threadneedle Street' is (behind the façade) in praise of the spider. These life-force markets are where those vying for 'the mark of Marduk' gather to offer their oblations, bids, for the blessings of Mammon, Marduk. From these relay stations *all* the wealth of the world is sent to the spider to distribute, according to their obligations and influence, among the *Elite* on Earth.

The Moonopoly Rituals

Moon-ship Sin became the great 'harvester of souls' designed to keep humanity enslaved to the sphere of control imposed by Naga and his hierarchy. From the great dragon queen Ninurtra, down to her priestly class on Earth, 'wicked and vile' ceremonies were performed in her honour. Unknown to the masses, carried out under the darkness of the Moon Sin. Horrific rituals were performed to feed this Serpent Queen's thirst for blood and sacrifice. The colours black and red were used all over the Earth to represent the Elite order of Naga and Ninurtra (both Saturn and Moon). The Velon and Archons demanded death in all its forms and therefore 'death' became the 'focus for life' on Earth. 'Fear of death' was the ulti-

PAY DAY

WORK
Careers/ Uniforms
15

Bank Holidays
16

VOTE
Politics
17

Pensions / Insurance
18

DEATH

Christmas **13**

Halloween **12**

EASTER **11**

INCOME TAX

Credit **9**

Savings & Loans **8**

Goods & Services **7**
1971619

Cashless Society **666**

Go to Jail

WOMAN

MOONOPOLY

MAN

Global Government **20**

Global Religions **21**

Global Media **22**

CARBON TAX

Legal System **24**

War & Arms **25**

Big Pharma **26**

Property & Land **27**

Education **5**

Television / Computers **4**

Parents / Nanny State **3**

Birth Certificate **2**

BIRTH
GO

Vile ceremonies dedicated to Ninurtra.

Naga-Kronos symbolism behind *all* religions.

The Velon (Archon) feed off death and destruction in *all* its forms.

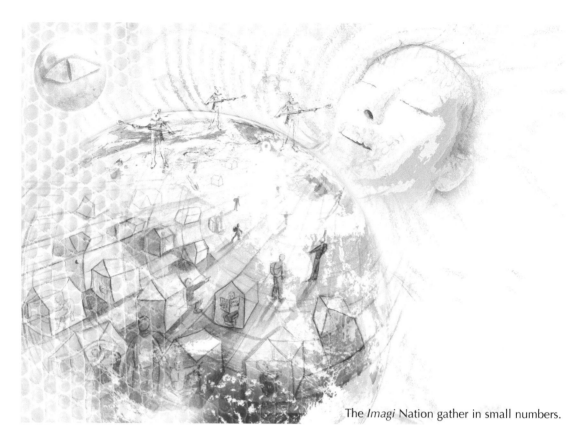

The *Imagi* Nation gather in small numbers.

mate form of control and therefore the dead carried the living on their backs everyday. War, bestiality, sacrifice, pain, injustice and even insanity were a few of the many symptoms of the disease and disorder that had now infested the *new* 'fake' Earth.

Over time Marduk's Earth became known as Global Babylon, a 'game-world' reality and its symbol was the 'all-seeing eye' of Naga. A 'new world order' had been set in motion. A sophisticated regulation system, 'artificial time' was implemented for everyone to abide by. So cleverly woven in with the matrix was it that nobody questioned it. It was accepted as life, as *'reality'*. TV, Jobs, roles and fake realities became an addiction for humans in Marduk's matrix. The game of 'time' and 'Sin' (Saturn and Moon control) now cemented in the human 'mind-body-spirit' meant that *all* had succumbed to the machine-world of 'death' and 'time'. With 'time' also came 'money' (or 'mooney'), perhaps the greatest form of control in Marduk's 'game-world reality'. Marduk commanded the game that ruled over the collective mind of those that now incarnated on Time-ship-Earth'... but as most games go, over time people grew weary of it. Some even began to see beyond it; past the 'tents of perception' they had pitched on this landscape of limitation. Over what would seem like 'the rise and fall' of many civilizations, a small group of humans had started to *remember* the source of their true creative power.

The *Imagi* Nation

Just a few, these humans dwelt on the 'outer rim' of Marduk's 'game-world' and could see beyond it. Incarnating in different epochs, and under different names throughout history and regions, the Gnostics, and the Cathars were among them. Now they were becoming known as the *Imagi* Nation. Small in number, but great in heart, they were rebels who beheld a distant light growing brighter a quickening vibration calling. The illusionary binds, Marduk's artifice were loosening. The gloom-cowl over the world was lifting.

The 'inner eye' of more and more of humanity was awakened and thence they realised how they had been living in an illusion, a glass house', (a 'prison made of Naga's *false* light), constructed out of fear, death and 'time'. Like the flame of a candle burning, shining, this false light had held humanity, as moths are held against a window pane mesmerized by the light. Inevitably the hearts of the *Imagi* Nation turned to breaking free. Like a 'jack in a box', at any time soon, they were ready to spring from their 'boxes of control' into the real world beyond the false light imposed by the vile hierarchy of Naga.

The time had come for those that now could see the new light to act in defiance of those both visible and 'invisible' that desired suffering and tyranny at all costs. That act would bring their ancestors back to them, which *is* exactly what happened.

The Infinite

GALAXIES

Eye of the Goddess
Durga

Galaxy

Manu Galaxy

The Demiurge
Naga

SUNS & STARS

Stars Systems birthed

Star of Ammon

The Ancient Face

Ammon Becomes Saturn

Ninurtra
Reptilian Queen

SUNS

Jupiter

Archon

Comets

Sulis
Langa

Lions of Regal

Lord Marduk

Narashima of Regal

Cyborg Velon

The Children
of Narashima

Reptilian
Watchers

WANDERERS & SATELITES

Kokoro

Shaka

Lonza

Lion Priests
of Naga

Moon Ship

Priests of Jeal

Light to Shadow Moon Control

Narashima's People

The Veil - Ring Not Pass

Bone Men

Lion, Bear & Monkey
People

Black Armies of Saturn
The Illuminat

PLANETS

Sophia - Manu's Daughter

Bad Copy of Sophia

False Earth

The Matrix
Illusionary 4th World

Portals

Original Humans
of the Original Earth

© Neil Hague 201

Part Four: THE AWAKENING

2000 AD to ...

*"The Sun will be darkened and the Moon will not give its light, the stars will
fall from the sky and the heavens bodes will be shaken.
The sign of the Son of man will appear in the sky"*

Mathew 24:15

*"The Full Moon at night over the great mountain, the wise man with his
brain undivided has seen it. Invited by his disciples to become immortal,
his eyes to the south, his hands and body amid the fire"*

Nostradamus Century 4:31

The Goddess Durga now stirred. The great Lions of Regal would rise with her.

On a distant star and within our Galaxy, those gathering on Earth felt a change, a shift in vibration; a cry streaking out from the deep, throughout every neuron of the wilderness. The *Imagi* Nation had heard it. Intuitively they sensed the true 'logos' returning and with it their original home. The Universe had awoken. It had slept for aeons.

A great lion awoke to a distant sound', a 'vibration' echoing through the void. She too had now heard the voice beckoning the dawn that had illuminated the mind's eye of the gathering *Imagi* Nation but now her people were calling her too. Increasingly upon Earth the collective light of the people had begun to blaze as they recalled the true light of their original Sun and the fire that connected Ammon to their hearts. The Goddess Durga now stirred. The great Lions of Regal would rise with her.

A star was moving from the centre of our Galaxy. More like a comet sent from the heart of the Lioness, this comet was a ball of energy that contained the form of Manu and the fire that was originally taken by Naga. Durga had answered the call of those on Earth whose hearts desired to return to the Golden Age of Sophia. As the comet moved through our Galaxy the watchers, sky gazers and those that dreamed of the world before the 'fall' saw its trail of fire pass across the Heavens. To them it was a sign that Naga's time was coming to end!

As the light of this star passed though space and time it awoke the sleeping giants of Regal, a star system that was the home of the Lion Gods. These mighty lions had remained asleep in their abode since before the time of Ammon. The lions were the direct descendants of Durga and were woken by her as the comet passed through the 'wormhole' that connected Regal with

The star of Durga heads for Regal and Shekena.

Shekena – our Solar System. The lions would be roused now that humanity had called on their ancestral inner power beckoning these lions home to the *Imagi* Nation. The first to awake was Narashima the 'old one' followed by Shaka and Kokoro. As the lions stirred, Narashima sought council from Manu taking his staff he gathered the wisdom of the original source of power, the star of Durga. Now carrying the power he took the light of the star of Durga, placed it on his staff and with it signalled to the lions of Regal. The light from Narashima's crystal also found Lonza who had been in hiding since the time of the original battles for Earth. Lonza lit up his body suit with the light of the crystals of Durga and prepared for the coming battle for Earth.

Legends say that when all three lions woke, fear would depart from humanity and the 'eye of the heart' would be carried within all those that remembered their true source of origin - *Oneness*.

The lions had emerged from hiding and gathered at the edge of Shekena, the place where the roots of the Solar Tree meet it's branches. With great speed and power they moved towards the Earth, the home of their ancestors. They poured through the portal of the Sun called Sulis, created by the 'solar torch' left by Naga, flooding the night with the energy of their home star. The *Imagi* Nation had now grown in large numbers to meet the Lions of Regal on a subconscious level. So as Narashima's energy passed throughout Shekena's domain, a great battle in the Solar Tree ensued. The coming of the

Narashima consults Manu.

Lonza activates his crystal suit.

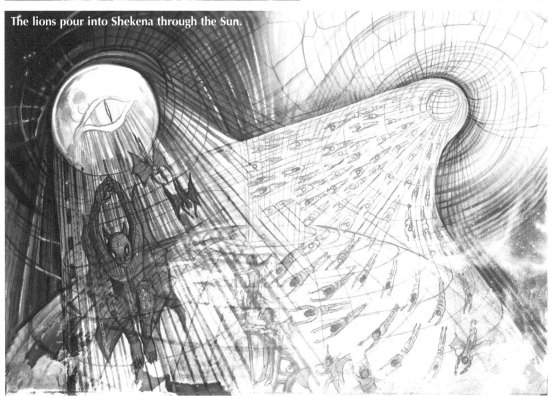

The lions pour into Shekena through the Sun.

Exorcising the Moon.

lions woke even more humans, many that had slept for far too long were now able to see the light of the 'truth vibration' as it rose upwards and filled the skies. A tidal wave of consciousness was massing inside the Earth's magnetic sphere and Naga's demons or Velons could not stop the coming wave of this higher vibration. For all of their control, (blueprints of the mind), the Velons/Archons and their machines did not see the advancing lions. Fixed only on keeping humanity in a 'limited box of perception', the advancing 'light of the lions' came too quick and was beyond their 'sight' and power.

The giant Narashima moved on the Moon while his brothers led an army of 'lions' straight into the heart of Naga's Earth matrix. Narashima then took the form of a blue lion. Gathering the space between the Sun and the Earth, and using the plasma

and energy from the centre of the Galaxy he grew in size. Infused with the leonine aspect of Manu he transformed into a solar lion and flanked by the lions of the goddess Durga he opened his jaws swallowing the Moon-ship Sin whole. For those on Earth that witnessed this event, the full Moon, in a cloudless sky 'disappeared' instantly and returned not white, but with the colour of the Sun. The Moon had been 'torched'. This became known as the 'slaying of the Moon' a 'signal in the sky' that would 'speed up' human evolution and remove the binds of 'time'. Without the binds of the calendar, the clock and the calculating regimes of Marduk nature allowed that every human could access both their past and future selves to 'tune into' the time before Sin. In an instant the Matrix was unlocked and all of the 'demons' that had attached themselves to the Moon-ship were banished by the light of the Star of Regal.

Narashima swallows Moon-ship Sin.

Narashima passed through the 'bright white stone' expelling the Serpent Queen, removing her possession over it. The 'stone' was now set free from Naga's grasp and became a pure 'stone in the Solar Tree. With the Moon now cleansed, the lions entered the Earth Matrix, which was now free from the Moon's control (the 'Moonopoly game' board), forcing Naga to *release* its hold over humanity.

An ocean of energy became a vast tidal wave, turning, rising, it gathered more human-lions focused in their 'perception' of all that had to be done to free the Earth from its imprisonment. Humanity, now liberated from the Moon's control, had truly awoken. For everyone that woke up another lion would join the ranks of this growing wave coming through the portal of the Sun. With clear sight and remembering of who they were, (and with the aim of a warrior of

Kokoro arrives on the 'Roof of the World' and shatters the 'invisible prison'.

Shaka and the Lion Army enter N_____ 'Matrix' casting _____ demons.

A golden orb filled with the Lions of Durga descends on the Earth, while Manu stands in the doorway between both worlds.

light), these lions rained down on the glass roof of the Earth Matrix.

The roof of the world trembled, it cracked... and in came Kokoro. With one clean command of his staff, Kokoro stamped out the demon hoards that hovered above the roof of the world. The blast from his staff was so strong that, from the crystal at the top, the light of Manu burst out, and radiating like the beam of a lighthouse, shone its brilliance for everyone who still needed to see the darkness around them. In an instant all that was hidden was revealed, and the illusionary world became apparent for what it was – a prison for the soul. As more lions poured in, Shaka led an army of lions into

Narashima and Lonza banish Naga and his demons.

Narashima rips the veil and exposes the wicked ceremonies of Naga's priests on Earth.

the centre of the Earth Matrix in full view of Marduk, casting out demons as they went. Narashima then ripped the veil between all that is hidden from public view and the 'inner sanctum' of Naga's 'secret world'. In an instant the priests of Naga were stopped from adorning their master, through their 'machines of wickedness'. Scattering like rats in a

farmer's barn once the door is opened, consumed by the light of 'truth'; they had nowhere to run. Justice would be done! Above the Earth a golden globe was now descending. An orb filled with the faces of the Lions of Durga, massing and waiting to raise the Earth Matrix to its original state. Manu stood in the doorway between two worlds enacting the 'opening of the doors of perception'. As the giant lions entered the matrix, scattering more of Naga's minions, Kokoro moved amongst the people of

Earth touching them with his words and his light. He was heading for the heart of Marduk (see *Kokoro - The Rise of the True Human Being*). While his brother Narashima (now in full form and aided by Lonza), banished more Demons and Velons in full view of the all-seeing eye of Naga. Now 'exposed' Naga's full body was stretched out from the Moon (left) and the *Imagi* Nation and human lions stood in defiance against all that this red serpent had brought to their world. No longer would

they comply! With one final act Narashima then took the light of Manu and 'paraded' it over the surface of the Earth. So intense was the light of Manu that when Naga looked upon it he was instantly struck blind in his 'third eye'; the incinerator that cast all of his magic was extinguished. His infernal reign of terror was at an end.

With this final act a great cheer went up all across the world and humans came together everywhere, as they had in the Golden Age, to rejoice in their freedom.

Humans that had *remembered* their true power were 'transformed' into lions on Earth with expanded minds - above the 'prison fear frequency'. With the fall of the 'matrix of control' so great was the rise in consciousness of the Earth that it was seen from outside as a gigantic encircling 'force field', in the form of a celestial lion. The ancestors had returned.

Humans 'become' Lions as they break out of the 'matrix of control'.

The Celestial Lion engulfs the Earth.

A 'new era' had dawned. The Age of the Rainbow was born. And through the many generations that followed the great revival…what became of the Earth? With the restored devotion of the humans that she had always so selflessly cared for, she blossomed again into the magnificent and vibrant golden orb she had been in ancient times; and now, unequalled in all of Creation, as a sanctuary of love, inspiration, and laughter.

THE END

"There will come a day when people of all races, colors, and creeds will put aside their differences. They will come together in love, joining hands in unification, to heal the Earth and all Her children. They will move over the Earth like a great Whirling Rainbow, bringing peace, understanding and healing everywhere they go. Many creatures thought to be extinct or mythical will resurface at this time; the great trees that perished will return almost overnight. All living things will flourish, drawing sustenance from the breast of our Mother, the Earth."

Navajo-Hopi Prophecy of the Whirling Rainbow

Glossary of Characters and Creatures

Ammon - The 'Sun that moved' into Shekena (the Solar Tree) and became the pivotal Sun and *light* for Sophia.

Black Army of Kronos - Genetically made on Kronos by the Velon, these 'jet black' (beetle-like) biped figures are used by the velon to invade planets. The Bone Men usually lead them. Every 'police state' on 'planets taken' would be modelled on the Black Army.

Bone Men - All white skeleton-like figures over two meter high. From the Orion constellation, they uphold the invading hierarchy.

Durga - The eye of the Universe, a Lion Goddess that gives life to all galaxies.

Fire Stones - The source of Durga's ability to 'give life' and 'create galaxies'. In the hands of a creator God (like Naga), they can be used to wreak havoc and destroy worlds.

First People - The original (aboriginal) humans that populated Sophia. The interbreeding of these people with 'star people' created tribes such as the Dogon, the Hopi and the Aborigines.

Giants of Orion - Green and white deities that attacked Sophia but were defeated by the Simus Bear People. Some Orion tribes eventyally inhabited the planet Mars. They 'seeded' the Egyptian and Sumerian Dynasties after the Flood.

House of Marduk - The 'Elite' on Naga's *new* Earth that maintain the 'imposition' and 'tyranny' of Marduk, while worshipping Naga through vile ceremonies in secret.

***Imagi* Nation** - A small group of humans that have gathered in 'remembrance' of their 'original home' and memory of the *'Oneness'* that brought them into the Universe.

Infinite Consciousness - The 'self aware', 'formless', 'all-knowing' *source* that created Durga.

Jeal - Wolf men taken from the star Sirius B. Tortured by Ninurtra's reptilian warriors of Draco in the battle for Shekena, they administer the new genetically modified human 'called Adam and Eve'.

Kilipoth - The 'ring makers' of Kronos, a giant cyborg race of machines that were created by Naga and travel in huge space ships.

Kokoro - The young lion of Regal. The smallest of the three giant brothers, but a formidable force that dealt with Marduk in the 'end days', (see the *First book of Kokoro - The Rise of the True Human being*).

Langa - The First Sun, a female Sun connected to the constellation of the Pleiades and adored by Sophia and the 'first people'.

Lion & Bear Army - A confederation of tribes from Regal and Sophia that fought against the armies of Marduk when they invaded her after the Flood.

Lions of Regal - Giant golden lions that live in the 'tunnels' (wormholes) between the star system of Regal and Shekena.

Lonza - The Blue Monkey King, originally from the Pleiades but influenced by the Lions of Regal. The Simus tribes 'followed' Lonza all over the Earth at the time of the 'First World' before the flood.

Lord Marduk - The creation of the Velon and Naga. Marduk is the '*false* Father God figure' imposed on humanity. He rules over the Earth in its darkest times.

Manu - Our Galaxy, part Durga (lion), part 'divine human form'. The source of all Suns.

Moon-ship Sin - A satellite that was born of Kronos

and fought over by various star tribes. Eventually taken by Ninurtra and her Draco warriors the Moon-ship becomes a Ghost-Ship and a *portal* for Naga.

Moon Slayer - An event that takes place when a 'full moon' *suddenly disappears* due to the 'full force' of the rising vibrational armies of Regal. The Moon is *slayed* and the possession of the space-ship is ended by this event.

***Moon*opoly** - The creation of Marduk to keep humanity in servitude to 'time and money'. Moonarchs (or Monarchs) are connected to Marduk's game.

Naga (Demiurge) - Naga created the Demiurge (a living schism) out of the 'theft' of the 'fire stones' of Durga. It became the driving force of Naga creating the *new* Earth Matrix that would replace Sophia.

Naga's Demons - Winged creatures that live on the 'roof of the world' and on the Moon. They attach themselves to humans that have emersed themselves in Marduk's Game *Reality*.

Naga's *New* Earth (Matrix) - The 'fake copy' of Sophia, that looks similar to the orignal Earth, but is illusionary and holds humanity in spiritual, mental and emotional chains.

Narashima - The elder lion and the oldest of the three brothers. He is able to change form and become different aspects of Manu.

Ninurtra - The cruel daughter of Naga and one of the three Draco 'gods' created by Naga when he first emerged in the 'time of creation'. The Draco have waged war against hunanity for millenia.

Pleiadians - Both bird-like and human, a species that occupy seven stars near Shekena. The Pleiadians are at war with the Draco and Lyrians since their star Alcyone was invaded.

Red & Green Lion Priests - Lions that converted to the 'ways of Naga' and now organise the Jeal.

Saturn - Another name for Kronos and a name that is used by the Elite on Naga's *new* Earth.

Shaka - Brother of Kokoro and a magician. He led an army of lions into Naga's Matrix and fought Naga's demons in the 'end days'.

Shekena (Solar Tree) - Another name for our Solar System a creation of Manu. Naga effects Shekena's body when he 'possesses' Ammon and brings the fire stone to the tree.

Simus Bear Tribes - One of the original species of Sophia and her protectors. Seeded on Ursa Major, they worshipped Langa and Lonza.

Sophia - The original name for Earth created by Naga at the beginning of creation.

Sulis - The new Sun (our Sun today) that was created out of Naga's 'torch' when he stole the fire stone of Durga and brought it into Shekena.

The Flood - A Great Deluge that was caused by the movement of Moon-ship Sin as it entered Sophia's domain. An event recorded all over the Earth.

Time of Creation - The period when Durga gave life to Manu and Manu 'doubted' his own ability to 'create'. Also called the 'splitting of the divine being'.

Truth Vibrations - A term used to symbolize the 'rising consciousness' of humans on Earth.

Urza - A planet and dwarf star that is the home of the 'eagles of Uthorna'. They fought the Kilipoth and Velon when Sulis and Urza clashed at the 'time of the creation' of Kronos'. (They will feature heavily in the *Third Book of Kokoro*, not yet published).

Velon (Archon) - A part-cyborg, part-reptilian species created by Naga when he created the Demiurge, possessed Ammon and created Kronos.

For all of Neil's books and imagery visit;
www.neilhague.com

Milton Keynes UK
Ingram Content Group UK Ltd.
UKHW051237060624
443694UK00003BA/22